Dedicated to...

With the blessings of
करुणावतारम्
Shiva
May your boundless compassion fill our
hearts with kindness, love, and peace

All the parents who try to
do their best for children

Nick and Mia wondered if Mama's favourite words were *Hurry Up!*

"*Hurry Up!* You are going to be late for school,"
Mama yelled in her SUPER urgent voice.

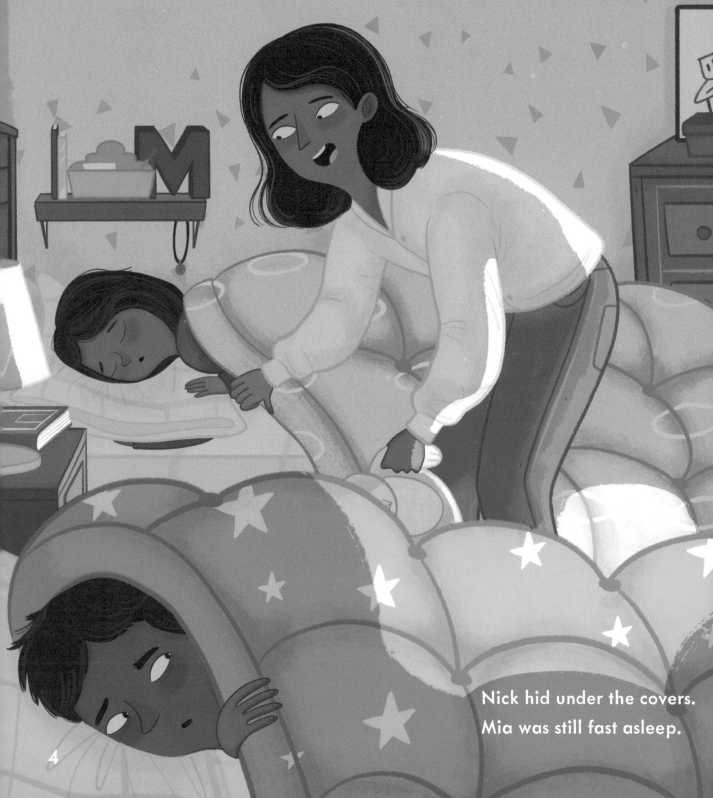

Nick hid under the covers.
Mia was still fast asleep.

4

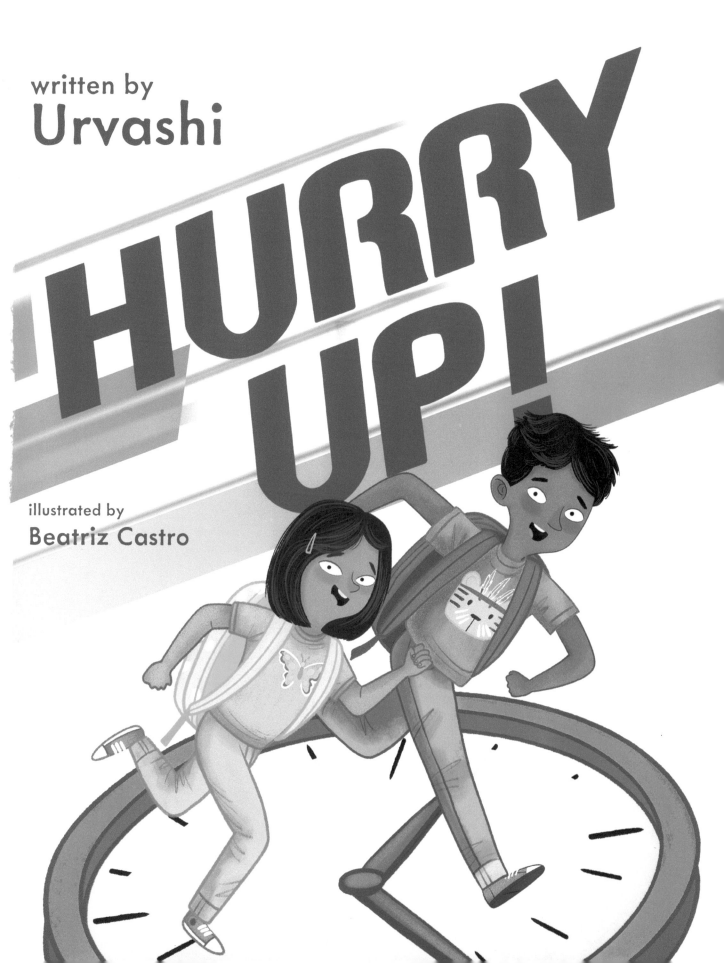

written by
Urvashi

illustrated by
Beatriz Castro

Mama, in her SUPER efficient style, tugged at Mia's blanket while picking up her stuffie.

"Hurry Up!" Mama shouted. "Get dressed!"

"Hurry Up! Finish your breakfast," said Mama in a SUPER charged voice.

Nick gobbled the cereal in his bowl. Mia stuffed the sandwich in her mouth.

Mama rushed them out the door. *"Hurry Up!"*

Nick and Mia stalled and tried to get dad to play silly games. Dad grinned as he waved. He went right back to his computer screen looking SUPER focused.

"*Hurry Up!* Get into the car." Mama's SUPER impatient voice made Nick and Mia scramble.

"*Hurry Up!*" Mama repeated.

There was no time to enjoy the puddles.

In the backseat, Nick and Mia argued.

"Your school bag is crossing the boundary line," complained Nick.

"Your foot is touching mine." Mia turned away, sulking.

Mama SUPER ignored them.

It was a REGULAR day at school

spelling test...

numbers...

tag at recess...

10

art and crafts...

SUPER busy, but OK.

Playtime at the park was SUPER fun. Rio had brought their dog. Mia finally was brave enough to go down the BIG slide. Nick was in line for the swing. He waited and waited and when his turn was next...

"*Hurry Up!* We have to go home," Mama called in a SUPER abrupt voice.

Nick took three deep breaths and counted to ten. He tried to feel calmer.

"Hurry Up! We—"

Before Mama finished, Nick had a big MELTDOWN. He stomped his foot. "You don't want us to have fun!" Nick shouted. He sat on the ground with a thud and sobbed. "All you care about are your SUPER silly rules!"

Now Mia yelled, too. "You are always rushing us!"

"Home! Now!" said Mama in a SUPER commanding voice.

After supper, Nick and Mia could hear their parents SUPER faint voices in the next room.

"Maybe if we tried..."

"I need to slow down..."

"We should explain... "

"What don't they understand?" Nick complained. "All they have to do is stop saying *'Hurry Up'* so much!"

Mia finished her drawing and joined Nick as he built a treehouse. This was SUPER helpful as it gave them time to think.

Nick whispered, "Should we surprise them tomorrow with OPPOSITE DAY?"

Mia cheered up. "It was so much fun at school last week. A BIG YES!"

"*Hurry Up!* Time for bed," said Mama in a SUPER tired voice.

Nick and Mia made puppy eyes but could not convince Mama to read a bed time story. They were disappointed but soon drifted into sleep, dreaming of SUPER exciting things they had planned for tomorrow.

"*Hurry Up!* OPPOSITE DAY!"

"Wake Up, Mama! Wake Up, Dad!" sang Nick and Mia as they entered their parents' room, dressed in Mama's robe.

"*Hurry Up!* You are going to be late for your meetings," Nick said, sounding SUPER important.

Mama and Dad sat up rubbing their eyes, looking SUPER confused.

"*Hurry Up!* Make your bed!" Mia said in a SUPER responsible voice.

"**Hurry Up!** Finish your breakfast. Sugary cereal is good for you," said Nick.

Mia explained in her SUPER knowledgeable voice, "Your plate should have foods of many colours, just like the rainbow." She scooped vegetables and fruit onto her plate.

"What's going on?" Mama finally asked, sounding SUPER intrigued.

Nick and Mia laughed.
"It's OPPOSITE DAY! Now *Hurry Up!*"

"Race to the car!" Nick ordered.

As they ran past Dad, he said, SUPER playfully,
"Not so fast! If it's OPPOSITE DAY, what's the hurry?"

21

Nick held the car door open for Mama.
"Take your time. Enjoy the beautiful flowers in our garden."

In the backseat, Nick and Mia were SUPER polite.

"Here, let me help you with your school bag," offered Mia.

"I insist you choose the songs today," urged Nick.

Mama was SUPER amused.

It was a GREAT day
at school

spelling test...

numbers...

tag at recess...

24

art and crafts...

SUPER busy, but FUN.

Playtime at the park was SUPER SUPER fun. Rio's dog had learnt a new trick.

Mama got on the big slide.

"Careful! Hold on to the sides," said Mia in a SUPER experienced voice.

Then Mama was in line for the swing. She waited and waited and when her turn was next...

"Take your time," Nick called in a SUPER grown up voice.

But when Mama asked if she could go on the slide again, Nick said no. "We have to go home. Don't forget the rules! No more asking for extra playtime."

"Hurry Up, Mama!" Mia urged. "We have other fun things planned."

"That's right," Nick agreed. "We're walking home backwards!"

After supper, Nick and Mia used SUPER encouraging voices as they got their parents to do calming activities for the evening.

"You got this..."

"I like the choice of colours..."

"The red blocks could go here."

Everyone looked SUPER relaxed. And that's when Mama said, "Dad and I promise to stop yelling *'Hurry Up'* all the time."

"Woohoo!" Nick shouted and Mia broke into a happy dance.

"OPPOSITE DAY worked!"

29

"Time for bed," said Nick, waving Mama's favourite childhood book. He read the book in his best voice while Mia added the sound effects. Mama and Dad were SUPER entertained.

Nick and Mia tucked their parents into bed. "Sweet dreams," Mia whispered gently.

"Mia, let's watch TV now," said Nick SUPER casually.

"Hold your horses right there!" Mama said. "OPPOSITE DAY ends at bedtime!"

Nick and Mia sighed and walked very slowly to their own bedroom.

"Don't worry, Mia," Nick promised.
"OPPOSITE DAY ONCE AGAIN starts in the morning!"

Hurry Up! It's time to plan YOUR OPPOSITE DAY!

Dear Parents,

I was inspired to write this book when I heard my little ones say "Mama's favourite words are *Hurry Up!*" I realized how much I rushed them, as I juggled multiple responsibilities. I also realized how much they took it in their stride and had fun along the way. They are teens now, but my favourite words are probably the same: *Hurry Up!*

I wish you and your children moments of connection and fun. Reading together contributes to secure attachment. As you are probably well aware, kids love repetition and turn-taking. Enjoy!

With appreciation,

About the Author

Urvashi Sirohi Joseph, MA, MSW, RSW is a Registered Social Worker, Psychotherapist, and Clinical Supervisor based in the Greater Toronto Area. She is an enthusiastic writer with a love for adventure, fairy gardens, and all things creative. Urvashi hopes to spark joy, creativity, and connection in every reader.

🌐 www.psychotherapyandwellnessclinic.com

📷 @urvashi.author

About the Illustrator

Beatriz Castro is a professional illustrator. Growing up in Logroño, La Rioja, Spain, she was inspired by the natural world aroud her to draw and write fantastic stories. She is passionate about animals and books. She lives with her husband and their three dogs and two birds flying around the house.